A History of

Taree Scribblers

A writers' group of the Manning Valley

A History of Taree Scribblers

For information address mickiedaltonbooks@lycos.com

First Printing 2020

ISBN: 978-0-6485470-7-5

Published by The Mickie Dalton Foundation
NSW
Australia

A History of Taree Scribblers

2006 - 2007

After asking at Taree Library if there was a writers' group in the Manning area and finding there was none, Bob Winston left his phone number at the library to be contacted regarding any writers interested in forming a supportive writing group. Narida Bell subsequently rang Bob and they met over coffee, the first informal meeting of Taree Scribblers.

The first formal meeting was held in the committee room of Taree Council Chambers and the name Scribblers was chosen for the group. Bob then placed an advertisement in the Manning River Times, inviting interested writers to come to the next meeting. The following meeting more than tripled the size of the fledgling writing group.

Early meetings were held on a Tuesday morning but this changed to the second Wednesday of the month and when the new Taree Library was finished the Scribblers were given a permanent meeting room at the back of the library.

For the first couple of years, Scribblers had a steady membership of about half a dozen and meetings revolved around the readings of members' written works. Prompt words were issued each month to inspire new short stories and poems and members exchanged tips and tricks on writing.

2008

The Manning Valley Winter Festival in 2008 provided the first platform for Scribblers members to have their work heard by the public. A Prose and Poetry Dinner was held in the Lilli Pilli Restaurant, at the Casuarina Motel in Cundletown. Scribblers read their work to diners between courses and Narida Bell provided some fine jazz singing for entertainment.

Beginning in 2008, Scribblers awarded cash prizes to talented creative writing students from Chatham, Wingham and Taree High Schools. This continued for three years.

Les Murray was our first guest speaker. He gave a very interesting talk on the sources of his inspiration and how his poetry has changed over his lifetime.

2009

Several Scribblers members attended a weekend Creative Writing Retreat given by Mary White at Hidden Valley, near John's River.

2010

Scribblers' first anthology Scribbles was published in 2010, containing stories, poems and memoirs as well as some very fine cartoons drawn by Fanny Matuta. With an editorial committee of five members, the book took six months to write and edit. The photograph of the Scribbly Gum trunk for the cover was taken by John Davies. Peter Loveday was responsible for publishing the anthology which was launched at the Taree Art Gallery during the Manning Valley Winter Festival in July. One of our members, Elizabeth Christo, managed to rustle up some fine food and wine from sponsors, who included Great Lakes Wines, Comboyne Cheeses, Saxbys Softdrinks and Rudi Mentges Master Meats. A celebration cake was topped with an icing facsimile of the book cover. Fanny Matuta made dozens of giveaway bookmarks, each with a copy of one of her cartoons.

Scribblers members managed to sell over 200 copies of the anthology, including through local outlets such as Angus & Robertson Taree, Books Two Wingham, Artisans Retreat Tinonee and All About Arts and Framing Taree.

As well as continuing with Tips & Tricks and the choosing of prompt words each month, Scribblers meetings still opened with a reading of members' works, usually inspired by the prompt word. This activity has proved to be an invaluable support to the writers right up to the present day.

During these early years, Scribblers meetings often included a Writer's Digest, in which a member reviewed for the group a book they had read. Different members of Scribblers gave mini workshops as well, to help improve writing skills.

2011

Scribblers members took on the ambitious task of writing a progressive novel in the first half of 2011. The novel was called The Retreat. Different members took turns each month to write successive chapters of the novel. Though the end result was a bit of a muddled mess, the exercise was useful for learning to write longer works with a single main character and conflict. It was quite a challenge to incorporate each member's monthly contributions to plot and character.

2012

As part of the Manning Winter Festival, Scribblers members had stories and poems published in The Manning River Times for six weeks in June/July. Also for the festival, Bob Winston collected stories and poems from local school children and posted them in shop windows for public view.

John Davies assisted with a poetry-in-the-street project, in which excerpts from famous Australian poems were placed in shop windows throughout Taree.

Timothy Daly travelled up from Sydney to Taree to give an in depth talk on writing plays to Scribblers in 2012.

2013 - 2015

Scribblers continued to grow in membership over these years. Some members dropped out due to ill health and others moved away from the area. All were sadly missed by those still in the group. However, new writers often came along to meetings to try out Scribblers for size and quite a few ended up staying.

In 2015, Scribblers combined with Taree Artists Inc for a major project called Duets in Paint & Print. Scribblers members each wrote a story or poem and these were given to the artists to inspire new paintings. In turn, the painters brought paintings and these were given to the writers to inspire new stories and poems. The project culminated in a month-long exhibition at the Bean Bar Café and Harrington Library, in which the paintings were hung beside their accompanying written works. A number of paintings were sold, along with their story or poem. All members agreed it had been a worthwhile exercise to push their writing into new areas and to higher standards.

In 2013, guest speaker Caroline Rhodes gave a talk on writing monologue. Also in 2013 and again in 2015, Wiriya Sati, the Mid North Coast producer from ABC Open, visited Scribblers to give workshops on short story and writing for ABC Open.

In 2015, Scribblers set up a closed Facebook page to share documents and writing support for each other. It allows members to stay in touch between monthly meetings and to upload helpful websites and information for each other. The page also has Scribblers documents and contact lists uploaded so all members can have access.

Also in 2015, the running organisation of Scribblers was formalised with elected committee positions which included Chairman, Treasurer and Secretary. Positions are vacated at the end of each calendar year and new members elected or previous members reconfirmed at the February meeting.

2016

Quartets in Paint & Print was the follow-up project from the previous year's collaboration with Taree Artists Inc. Scribblers member Joy Cooksey and Taree Artists member Lyn Bemet were the inspiration, and Joy did most of the organising for the project after Lyn became ill. For this project, there were seven groups of writers and artists from A to G. Each group comprised two writers and two artists. Each writer in the group penned the first paragraph of a story or poem then gave it to their partner to finish. Each artist in that group then painted a portrayal from one of the pieces of writing. Each artist in the group also painted 10% of a canvas then gave it to their partner to finish. These paintings were then handed to the two writers in the group, one each, to complete their own poem or prose inspired by the painting. The Bean Bar hosted the month-long exhibition once again.

This same year, Scribblers published a book of the Duets in Paint & Print from 2015. Joy Cooksey and Lyn Bemet were the inspiration for this project and covered the organisation of it. A friend of Joy's, Ashley Cleaver, was kind enough to take quality photos of the paintings. Joy and Lyn then assembled the information of the photos and writing to pass on. Jacqui Winn did the copyediting and with Gary Taaffe, helped organise the book ready for printing. Gary also undertook the publishing task and what was produced was a beautiful book with colour plates of the paintings and their accompanying writing.

The end of 2016 saw the inaugural Scribblers Writing Competition, in which members submit a story or poem from one of the monthly writing tasks. The competition is judged by someone from outside the group and the winner and three place-getters were awarded prize certificates at the annual Christmas Party in December.

2017-2018

Scribblers expanded in size over these years and often struggled to fit into the library meeting room.

A Scribblers brochure was produced by Gary Taaffe, so newcomers and the wider community could be given information about the group. Gary also established a Blast List – a handy email list so that members could send an email to all members when needed. An information pack was put together in 2018. It contained a guide for new members, a brochure and a contact details form.

Sadly, two of our much-loved members died in 2018. Jack Noble was only nineteen years old but he made an enormous impact on the group, with his intelligence and humour. In spite of significant disability, he had published a book of poetry and continued to write entertaining and thought-provoking works while he was with us. Jo Stratmoen also died unexpectedly in 2018. She had been a member for several years but had lived in Sydney over recent years. She was a talented writer of television scripts and short stories.

In 2017, movie agent Alan Harkness gave a talk to Scribblers on the movie industry in Australia. In 2018, Marcus Dabb gave a workshop on Life Writing, which inspired many Scribblers to dive into writing their own life stories.

2019

Monte Dwyer, well-know travelogue writer for television was scheduled to give a presentation on his travels in the Red Centre in the November meeting. However, that was during the intense outbreak of bush fires throughout the eastern part of Australia with many severe fires breaking out close to Taree. At one point, the Pacific Highway south of Taree was closed and many areas around were threatened. In the week of our scheduled meeting, the library was closed, together with all other municipal buildings and our meeting was cancelled.

Monte was still able to be the judge of our Prose and Poetry competition and the results are posted elsewhere in this book.

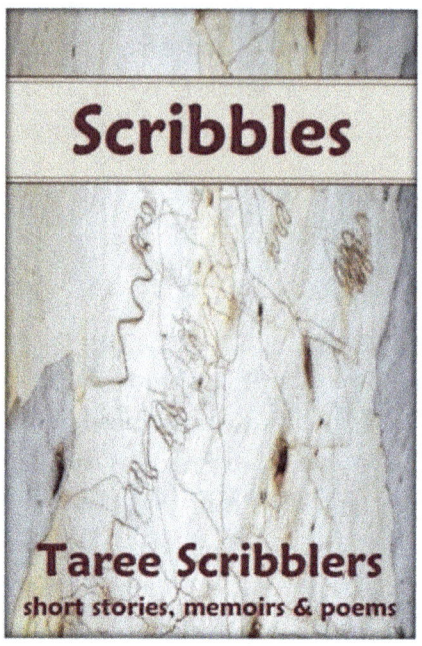

Published in 2010, this fine anthology by the writers of Taree Scribblers promises plenty of laughs, some poignant moments and the occasional surprise. Short stories, memoirs, poems and cartoons showcase the broad talents of nine authors. The variety of their work is bound to give hours of satisfying reading.

"A scribbler is a free spirit, scribbling for love of word, tapping into that deep intuitive part of the artist. This published work has been laid bare, examined and edited. I do love a published work, the scribbler's full-stop. Viva Scribblers!"

Stephen Michael King

Published in 2016, *"Duets in Paint and Print"* is a collaboration between Taree Scribblers and Taree Artists, Inc., which resulted in a month-long public exhibition in Taree. Each duet of painting plus story/poem conveys much more than the sum of its parts and many visitors to the exhibition were fascinated by the creative interpretations.

Paintings inspired by written works occupy the first part of the book while the second part showcases written works inspired by the paintings.

The Things We Do

Monthly prompt words
Vocabulary exercises
Tips and Tricks
Guest speakers
Writers Digest, review of books
Stories and poems read aloud each month by members
Workshops given by Scribblers members
Annual in-house writing competition for members
Publish anthologies – two, at least!

Guest Speakers at Scribblers

Stephen Michael King, Children's Books
Les Murray, Poetry
Timothy Daly, Playwrighting
Caroline Rhodes, Writing Monologue
Wiriya Sati, ABC Open
Alan Harkness, Movie agent
Marcus Dabb, Life Writing
Monte Dwyer, The Red Centre (moved to 2020)

Special Scribblers' Projects

Prose and Poetry Dinner at Lilli Pilli Restaurant
Publishing the book: Scribbles
Duets in Paint & Print
Publishing the book: Duets in Paint and Print
Quartets in Paint and Print
Progressive Novel: The Retreat
Members' stories & poems in Manning River Times
Writing Awards presented to students at Chatham, Taree and Wingham High Schools

Winners of the Annual Scribblers Writing Competition

2016

1st Place: Heather Bolstler – "Heebie Jeebies"
2nd Place: Gary Taaffe – "Little Johnnie Galah"
Highly Commended: Kerry MacAulay – "Black Dog"
Highly Commended: - Robin Sheppard – "Your Frustrated Nightmare"

2017

1st Place: Terry Stanton – "He Can't Do That"
2nd Place: Michael Davies – "The Time of the Snakes"
Highly Commended – Gary Taaffe – "Chang's Lament"
Highly Commended: Maureen Larter – "Snakes"

2018

1st Place: Kerry MacAulay – "Cherie"
2nd Place: Heather Bolstler – "Chalcedony. That's You"
Highly Commended: Jenny Trotter – "Crickets"
Highly Commended: Barbara Edmunds – "Life's Dream"

2019

Two sections were included for 2019; one for Prose and one for Poetry

Prose

1st Place: Joy Cooksey – "Gods and Anti-Gods"
2nd Place: Desley Polmear – "Forever Waiting"
Highly Commended: Kerry MacAulay – "The King and the Perfect Horse"
Highly Commended: Robin Sheppard – "A Sigh for Destiny"

Poetry

1st Place: Joy Cooksey – "Citiscape"
2nd Place: Eve Grzybowski – "Dried Flowers"
Highly Commended: Jenny Trotter – "Time"
Highly Commended: Robin Sheppard – "Thunderstorm"

The Winners of the 2019 Annual Scribblers Writing Competition

The Prose Competition

1st Place – Joy Cooksey

Gods and Antigods

'I can't do that sir. It wouldn't be right.'

Her politeness is admirable, but the judge is unaware of the restraint behind her words.

They have not met before. He has no knowledge of her extensive repertoire of expletives.

'And why wouldn't it be right?'

'it would be very dishonest sir. I don't believe in God.'

He wavers protocol and orders the proceedings to continue. There is a very clear picture of events. Their goose is already cooked.

The judge keeps Kylie to 'Yes' and 'No' answers. His questioning is swift and concise. He has dealt with her type before and leaves her no room for argument. The hearing proceeds without further incident. He looks relieved, and a little pleased, as he sends her back to sit with her mother. Jason is called.

Like Kylie, he hides insecurity behind a show of indignant defiance at their unwarranted persecution. But in Jason's eyes there is a glint of fear. Unlike the notorious Kylie, he hasn't been in this much trouble before and he is scared.

'And Jason I suppose you don't believe in God either.'

Jason stares at his hands and ponders the question.

'Well some days I do, and some days I don't sir. That day we let down the tyres and trashed Mr Robinson's car was one of those days I was sure there wasn't a God.'

The judicial mask remains blank. 'Tell me what happened.'

'Mr Robinson wasn't fair sir. It wasn't us that caused the fight. We were just trying to drag Justin out of it. It wasn't a fair fight. They were too big to be picking on someone as small as Justin. It wasn't us throwing the rocks that smashed the window. It was them.'

'What did Mr Robinson say when you told him?'

'He wouldn't listen. He just suspended Kylie and me. He wouldn't let us say anything. He got really mad when Kylie started yelling at him, especially when she called him a...'

'That's enough.'

'Sir, even you couldn't believe there is a God on those sorts of days. We reckoned no one else was going to sort out Mr Robinson so we did. Some had to sir.'

On the way home the parents are still unable to believe the outcome.

'I thought it would be much worse. A good behaviour bond and a share of the repair costs is very lenient.'

'It's enough though, to keep Jason out of trouble for quite a while. I'm not so sure about Kylie. She still seemed to believe she had done nothing wrong.'

Unbeknown to them, the Magistrate was having similar thoughts. He understood Jason's confusion. People like Mr Robinson made him question his own belief in God. He almost envied the kids the satisfaction they had in sorting him out.

Hopefully Jason wouldn't return, but if Kylie wasn't back again within six months he knew it would be time to re-evaluate his faith in God.

2nd Place – Desley Polmear

Forever Waiting

Grace Bellamy picked up the Tally-Ho papers that were half buried in the weeds by the tank stand and went inside. She'd kept her husband Silas's stew warm over a lidded saucepan of water the night before. She grabbed the pot and scraped the contents into the dog's bowl. The blue healers, Sip and Soda, were ten years old and they lay around at the front door more than help Silas work on the farm these days.

She peeled a banana and cut it into small pieces and layered it on top of her porridge. Sunlight bathed the room. As she ate she wondered about the whereabouts of her husband of thirty eight years, ol' Silas. He could be a cantankerous old bugger at times but she loved him. After all these years of marriage, she was used to the silence between the two of them each evening. It was habit now. She often wondered if it was the same for most long-term marriages. She remembered in the early days how her skin used to be on fire when he looked into her eyes and his hands caressed her, but she noticed Silas's eyesight changed a few years after their marriage.

She didn't feel like the same person now. No swinging her around the lounge room floor to the music, no more laughter, no more fun. Life was never what you wanted. Grace already knew that much. She smiled as her mind shifted on hearing the chirping of the birds in the background. She tied the apron around her waist and began to bake a cake for her granddaughters twenty first birthday party.

In all these years, the two of them had lived a frugal life on the farm. They'd kept it up, only now in semi-retirement it wasn't necessary. They'd done alright financially with the crops and cattle. She smiled as she thought about it. As most old folk knew, habits were hard to break.

The sound of tyres on the gravel path broke her thoughts. She peeped through the window to see a police car. She released her apron ties and ran out the front door. Ol' Silas with a cop either side headed towards her.

'Hello Grace,' said Sergeant Cliff Harris. 'Spent another night inside…he's been roughed up a bit but he'll live.' Silas shuffled past Grace, head down. 'Once he's cleaned up a bit I think he'll need a strong coffee and a bite to eat.'

'Thanks Cliff. I wonder when he'll wake up to the fact he's not twenty one anymore. Bloody fool, one of these days he won't make it home.' He tipped his hat, half smile.

Grace found her husband in the bathroom struggling to get his clothes off. She sat him on the stool and pulled his boots off then dragged his pants to the floor. Struggling, she put him under the warm shower and joined him. 'You ol' fool' she said, kissing his forehead.

Highly Commended – Kerry MacAulay

The King and the Perfect Horse

"Long live the king!"

The cry echoed around the town from the turret high on the tower. Mutterings and titters could be heard amongst the crowd gathering below. No enthusiastic cheering. No hats thrown in the air.

The king picked up his megaphone and tried again but the only response was a muffled booing.

"Then long live higher taxes," he grumbled to himself.

He called his court adviser.

"Bring me my horse. I must ride among the peasants to show them who rules this kingdom."

The sound of tiny clippetty-clops on cobblestones heralded the arrival of his horse. The king clambered onto its back, with a lift up from his advisers. But he was now looking directly at the man's crotch. Not a dignified position at all. If he were to make an impression on his people he needed to be looking down on them. Physically looking down.

"Search my kingdom for a horse worthy of a king," he ordered.

RRR

In the next town, a tall horse slouched in the corner of the yard. He was depressed. Others had been chosen for parade duty but he knew he would never fit the mould. He hated being the butt of everybody's jokes. He resented being so tightly folded when he slept. He needed to be able to stretch, to explore new horizons. He wanted to be valued for who he was.

"Hey! You! What's the weather like up there?"

The horse moaned sadly to himself. That was it. He was sick of being teased. He stepped over the stable fence and cantered down the road. To a new life.

RRR

Being the king's adviser was not an easy job. The king would not face the reality of being vertically challenged. His ego was huge, in inverse proportion to his height. In his mind's eye he was already superior to everyone else. He already looked down on his own subjects and even his favoured adviser. His request for a horse worthy of a king would have to be considered carefully.

The responses to the adviser's urgent advertisement for a royal horse came in thick and fast. One stable owner had the strongest horse. Another claimed the prettiest horse. A third had the best dancing horse. And so it went. None satisfied the king's adviser.

But as he wandered down the road in despair, the adviser was astounded to see what looked like a horse on stilts. Its head was held high in a regal manner. Its bearing was proud. It had an elegant, elongated step. The king's adviser hailed it politely.

RRR

The king was impatient. He was halfway down the steps of his tower when he heard the snort of a horse. He felt its breath on his arm. He turned and the horse was at his elbow. He reached out and clasped its bridle. He easily slipped his leg over the saddle and settled onto its back.

"Finally found the perfect horse," he whispered in its ear.

Highly Commended – Robin Sheppard

A Sigh for Destiny

The dark haired young man walked purposefully along the corridor of the intimidating structure. A fleeting thought whispered through his mind as he paused for a moment. Was this really to be his destiny? Then, once more, stepping through into the dull light of the temple, Callen was greeted by his Master.

"Welcome, my young apprentice," said the ageing man, bowing to him in the symbolic ritual greeting of the order.

Callen returned the salutation.

His teacher continued. "Are you ready to begin, my young apprentice?"

"Yes, Master," Callen replied, solemnly, and as they moved into the lesson room he noticed a small bug crawling on the floor.

"Today we will learn to touch another's thoughts. To begin, you must go into your mind and find calmness. Now, turn you thoughts inward, Callen."

"Yes, Master." The young man began concentrating, but his present thoughts disturbed him. "Master?" He said, looking up.

"Something is troubling you?"

"Yes. This lesson is a bit difficult."

"Why is that?" His Master asked.

"Well, I have these electronic games at home, and some of them are sort of… well… violent, and all that stuff from them is in here." Callen pointed to his head. "And… well…" he continued, "it's a bit challenging to find the calm right now."

"Is that so?" The Master raised his eyebrows, then his eyes narrowed and he stared intently at the young man, making Callen feel uncomfortable. "You know a young apprentice should not be playing that sort of stuff."

"Yes, Master." Callen lowered his eyes. "But sometimes I just need to relax," he continued. "I go to work and they drive me nuts there, and I have this urge to blow a couple of them out of the water, so to speak. So, I go home and blow people up on the electronic games. Then I feel better," he said, looking up with a wry smile.

The ancient teacher sighed, then paused, seemingly deep in thought. "Let us move on. Try to access a part of your mind that is more settled."

"Yes, Master." Callen shut his eyes in concentration, and then exclaimed, "I have it!"

"Now," his teacher continued, "you saw that tiny creature on the floor earlier?"

"Yes, Master."

"Try to reach out and touch its mind."

Callen concentrated harder. "Wow," he said, feeling its thoughts. His eyes opened and he looked to the Master. "It's just got a stupid scaly bug mind," he said, with exasperation.

"No." The ageing teacher redressed him. "That stupid scaly bug is an organism. You need to love all organisms. Now, tell me, how do you feel?"

"Like I could step on it," said Callen, wondering again about his destiny.

There was an audible sigh from the great Master. "We have much to do and you still have much to learn. You will never reach the light side if you continue to think like that." And the ancient Master, sighed again.

The Poetry Competition

1st Place – Joy Cooksey

Cityscape

From near the Harbour Bridge,
the city now, does like a vagrant,
shake off the grey blanket of night-time squalor, and greet the
morning air.
Fragile jacaranda blooms paint mottled patterns on lichen-
spotted rooves,
and replace 'Eternity' with drifts of mauve graffiti along car-
lined foot-paths.
Aging cracks and crevices cradle grime.
Pigeons plod, and seagulls swoop,
in endless combat over café crumbs.
Cool sunlight snakes silently down onto cluttered, noisy walk-
ways.
Vehicles vie for slivers of space. Wheels skid and screech
impatiently.
Flashing lights vie with mobile phones,
for the control of jostling pedestrians, and confused tourists.
Aging sandstone support sophisticated glass and steel,
as it stretches skyward, to rise beyond the meniscus of
pollution.
Marauding rats scuttle into the dark under-belly.
Recent-revellers, slink away to slumber,
cradled in the conformity and silent solitude of distant cul-de-
sacs,
far from the beating of the city-heart.
A vagrant wanders up from below the Bridge, shaking off the
shadows of night
and stops to bathe in the kaleidoscopic colours of the sun-lit
city.

2nd Place – Eve Grzybowski

Dried Flowers

The eucalypt flowers have long finished,
pushed along by the early spring arrival.

The drought played a trick.
A fast flowering in the gum forest.

Now, the gums are brown, brittle, barren.
Like stars burned bright before they die.

But the decorative garden, regularly watered,
is still prodigiously colourful.

The Pavonia in particular is a class act,
a leggy plant at two metres tall.

Verdant leaves have been sapped by The Dry.
Yet, its deep red flowers are still near perfect.

Have you seen the intricate flowers?
They look like tiny hibiscus blossoms.

A cup of red petal encloses the inner heart,
The protective dark grey bracts.

From these explode Carmen Miranda crowns,
Grape-like anthers with filaments of red stamen.

Dawn is when the honeyeaters snatch-and-go,
when the blossoms' gestalt is dewy moist.

Then the searing heat of another cloudless day
And we say, 'Another perfect day in paradise.'

Highly Commended – Robin Sheppard

Thunderstorm

Summers intensity spans the day
The humidity stifling and high
With heavy heat and shimmering air
And the presence of a storm close by

Brooding dark clouds now cover the west
Creeping forward to blacken the sky
As they build in the afternoon twilight
With massive cloudbanks piling on high

The echoing sounds of rumbling
Spread out and permeate the land
Like a fearsome advancing army
The storm moves in to begin its stand

As twilight descends with bright flashes
The sky streaks with a thousand white sparks
Then a noise like artillery thunders
Cowering all who live in its path

Trees bow before the on-rushing wind
As it swirls 'round in violent gusts
Raking the lands like an airstrike
With unforgiving and savage thrusts

Low in the sky hang icy grey clouds
Jagged hailstones come thundering down
Loud like bullets from soldiers' guns
As they hammer the defenceless ground

Tumbling from an immense cloudburst
Rain spills down on the land far below
Drowning a tired and weary battlefield
Flooding rivers till they overflow

With its wrath and energy waning
The skies open to the coming night
As the storm moves on into the east
Leaving beams of yellowish sunlight

Highly Commended – Jenny Trotter

Time

The past is gone — a vague dream.

The future is a void — empty and dark.

The present is an existence — nothing more.

❧ *Some Developments in Scribblers* ❧

Two projects were completed in 2019 after much deliberation.

The Scribblers Mug

Several design concepts were suggested and reviewed and the design by Jenny Trotter was unanimously selected. The mugs were made by a company in Wauchope.

The Scribblers Logo

The same design by Jenny was adopted as the new logo for communications.

❧ *Scribblers Past and Present* ❧

Jacqueline Allen	Sue Genereux	Jack Noble
Cate Bartlett	Eve Grzybowski	Maurice Olde
Debbie Bayliss	Mim Haigh	Victoria Perry
Joy Bell	Wendy Haynes	Desley Polmear
Narida Bell	Jill Harvey	Philip Rack
Heather Bolstler	Grace Heyer	Tony Scott
Rick Bolstler	Lorren Hill	Robin Sheppard
Joyce Bradney	Michael Hollingworth	Joan Stanfield
Avril Brown	Elizabeth Kempers	Terry Stanton
June Brown	Diane Kennedy	Jo Stratmoen
Christine Calabria	Stuart Kennedy	Katrina Strick
Elizabeth Christo	Maureen Larter	Gary Taaffe
Joy Cooksey	Kate Loveday	Lyn Taylor
Marilyn Connors	Peter Loveday	Georgie Tisdell
Peter Damen	Kerry MacAulay	Jenny Trotter
John Davies	John Macdonald	Pamela Walthridge
Michael Davies	Margy McDonald	Melanie Wass
Gloria Davidson	Sue McKenzie	Kerry Watson
Karen Derwent	Bob McMillan	Irene Whight
Raelee Diamond	Fanny Matuta	Lucy Weller
Les Eastaway	Mila Moscova	Bob Winston
Barbara Edmunds	Patricia Murphy	Jacqui Winn
Anna Featherstone	Denise Murray	
Keith Franks	Desley O'Farrell	

❧ *Club Officers* ❧

Chairman: 2015 to 2018 – Garry Taafe
2019 – Michael Davies
Secretary: 2015 to 2019 – Robin Sheppard
Treasurer: 2015 to 2019 – Maureen Larter

❧ *Some of the Books Produced by our Members* ❧

Eve Grzybowski

Eve Grzybowski has been teaching for 30-plus years, practising yoga continuously since 1971, and training yoga teachers since the mid-nineties. Besides yoga, writing is a passion. She has written two published books, many yoga-related articles, and her pet– *Yoga Suits Her* – a weekly blog. Her memoir is a work in progress. Eve has written a no-nonsense, jargon-free book on yoga for novices and those with experience, too. There are chapters on motivation, breathing techniques, getting started, and how to cope with stress in your daily life.

Michael Davies

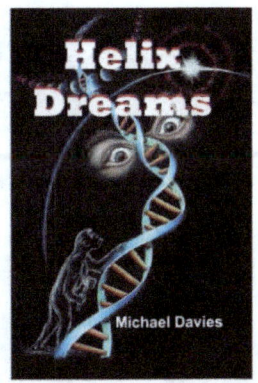

Michael has self-published 28 books. The *"Helix"* series will be complete with the third book in development at time of writing. Sixteen books have been written as collaborative projects with schoolchildren, like *"A Step Into the Past"* written with the students of Taree West Public School.

"The Janus Conspiracy" has been under review by a Hollywood producer as a possible political thriller movie project for some time. His other works include sci-fi, psychological thrillers, murder mysteries and espionage thrillers.

He has also published over eighty-five books for other writers.

Jacqui Winn

These award-winning short stories by Jacqueline Winn will have you laughing, crying and simply wondering at the extraordinary lives of ordinary people.

"Once More With Feeling" will take you on a journey of the imagination that celebrates the wonderful diversity of human life and cannot help but leave you looking at the world through different eyes.

"Salt & Pepper", Jacqueline Winn's second anthology is another rich assortment of short stories guaranteed to amuse one moment and touch the heart the next.

All of these stories have won awards in Australian, New Zealand, British and Irish literary competitions and have been published in anthologies and literary magazines all over the world. This is a collection sure to leave a lasting impression.

Les Eastaway

In September, 2010, the seed for this book was sown with the idea of penning a few lines following coffee and a chat about cricket. It was customary for Les to call in to Hurstville Oval (home of St George Cricket Club) and partake in a coffee with Taree old-boy Jon Jobson. Cricket and the good old days regularly surfaced in conversation.

Numerous visits to the Manning led to interviews and photographing ovals and grandstands, along with intense research at libraries and museums. Upper Lansdowne, Harrington, Moorland, Tinonee, Cundletown, Kimbriki, Wingham and Mount George were destinations that brought back memories of the old playing days and villages that provided both fine cricketers and honourable citizens.

Painstaking research has resulted in the statistics within, however it has been impossible to locate every item sought. Disposed of scorebooks and insufficient newspaper reports are common examples of missing information.

These few paragraphs outline the book briefly. The interviews, stories, laughter and hospitality have been one heck of a roller-coaster in this, the first book Les has compiled and published.

Jenny Trotter

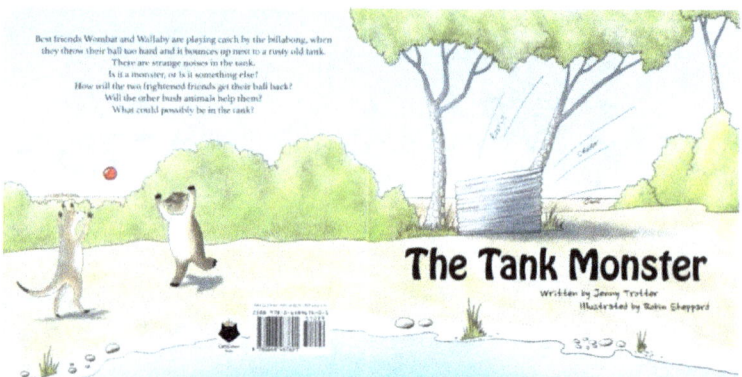

Jenny has had one short story published in the book titled- *"Duets in Paint and Print,"* published by Bunya Publishing, released 2016.

This is her first illustrated children's book. *"The Tank Monster."* It is published by CatNCrown Books, released 4th February 2019.

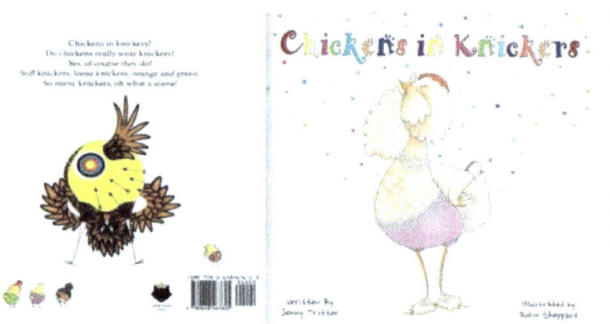

Jenny's second book, *"Chickens in Knickers"* was published on 2nd September, 2019.

At the time of writing, Jenny is also working on a full-length fantasy novel.

Maureen Larter

Maureen is a most prolific writer of children's book with over fifty published to date. She has also written a thriller for adults. *"Tarnished Gems"* which is highly popular.

Joan Stanfield

The four works published by Joan Stanfield. See her autobiography for descriptions of these books.

Some of the entries in "Duets in Paint and Print"

Painting by Robin Sheppard

"Shoot 'em, Johnny! Shoot 'em!"

He had a mare in his sights, the cross-hairs floating in front of her nose presenting the perfect shot.

"Don't let them get next door, Johnny or they're gone!"

BOOM! But he'd jerked the trigger in a panic. The bullet exploded a tree trunk to the left of the lead mare's head, wheeling them around in fright.

Johnny's dad smiled in satisfaction - he'd planned this hide perfectly. A camouflage net strung low between two shrubs across a trail regularly used by the brumbies. He knew they'd pull up at the blockage with their confusion presenting his son with ample opportunities to wipe them out.

"You'll get another shot, Johnny, just be cool."

You be cool, Johnny thought, frustrated over his dad breaking his concentration. He'd only agreed to come on this cull because he figured it would be his old man's last. He was so week these days that he couldn't even lift his own rifle. He put all the pressure on his son to finish off the last of the ferals from the high country but Johnny never really liked shooting them. He wasn't a cattle man or much of a shooter. It was his dad's passion, not his. Still, every moment with his dad was important to him now.

He tried to remain calm while working the bolt but it was sticky and wouldn't close.

"Come on, Johnny!"

He began to panic under the thunder of their hooves; the bolt rattling as he desperately tried to ram home another bullet. He looked up and saw the brumbies heading straight for them, his old man sitting tall and wild-eyed with excitement.

Right at the last second, Johnny closed the bolt and as he lifted the rifle, the bloody brumbies jumped the barrier. He threw himself to the ground and watched in horror as their hooves soured right over the top of him.

He spun around to follow up with a shot but as he got up, a flash of red caught his eye. It ran deep, all the way across his father's forehead, who now lay limp and lifeless at Johnny's feet.

Gary Taaffe, BunyaPublishing.com

Painting by Fred Bullen

Like a scar on the landscape the dirt road wove its way through the countryside. The threads of its colour meandering across the sides of hills till they were eaten up by its onward pursuit, then down it would plunge into the valley where its trail, like a long snake wandered its way through paddocks of grass that had gone to seed with the advancing of the seasons.

On it travelled towards its destination, momentarily halted by a causeway, where the water trickled over concrete that had been battered by years of floodwater filled with debris, driven by the rushing surge of the torrent from upstream.

The track resumed its winding way, it crossed the creek flats where the surface was peppered with wash rocks and stones that had rolled in bygone floods and been partly buried in silt. On it travelled beginning its climb upwards through the overhanging tree line, where the shadows were dappled with the sunlight.

Leaving the tree line and creek bed the road began to climb again making its way through open country. The road was dustier, dried by the sun in the hotter part of the year, the countryside looked up for welcoming rain that the season had not yet delivered.

The dusty road breached yet another rounded hilltop where it took in the surrounding landscape and its memories, stumps of long dead trees, fences with burn marks and wire in tatters, and an old farm shed with the roof partly caved in and left to the elements.

Still the road travelled on for its end was somewhere near beyond the trees in the distance. Ever closer it ran, back into the dappled shadows again, and there ahead this dirt road met its destination, a ribbon of black tar, the main road back to town.

By Robin Sheppard

Painting by Joy Cooksey

Is this a painting of a setting sun
With its glow spreading across the land
Or perhaps it's meant to be morning
With a beauty that could almost be grand

A ruggedness there in the dim twilight
Could be the remnants of a mountain side
Where cataclysmic events of another time
Have left scars that nothing could hide

An explosion perhaps of atomic scale
Shedding light on the land far below
Or perhaps it's just a gentle place
Where cattle and sheep might grow

Do I see trees on a hillside
Or rocks jutting out from its face
Where torrents of rain have washed it away
Or is this really an alien place

Clouds on the hilltop could be mist coming down
Or a storm brewing high in the sky
Do we really know what this painting is
Or has the artist played tricks without eyes?

By Robin Sheppard

Painting by Joy Cooksey

It sat amongst the darkness of the universe, open and bare to the wrath of its dying sun: once its saviour now a tormenter. Warm sunlight having long ago turned violent, burning away all traces of life.

A pale moon rose over blackened peaks, its light obscured by the toxic clouds that inhabited the skies, making its journey in silence as it gazed down across the broken and scarred landscape.

Through massive holes in the mountains, torn open by the ever-shifting earth, seeping magma cast its fiery glow upon the summits around it, as the volcanoes unleash their fury into the heavens.

Drowned out by the thundering landslides, the ghostly screams of the wind howled through the valleys, as if the souls of the long lost searched for peace, but had never found it.

Like jagged fingers reaching up, spires of rock exploded through the ground, grinding and screeching as it tore apart the outer crust, before once again collapsing beneath the surface as the violent earthquakes forced them to crumble down.

This was a doomed planet, near the end of its life, unable to save itself from the rage of its sun. Soon there would be nothing left, because for everything that begins, an end will surely follow.

By Jenny Trotter

Some Member Biographies

Jenny Trotter

Jenny cannot remember what sparked her love of writing, but she has always loved the characters and worlds of other authors, and thus began to create her own, which she continues to do so to this day.

Rick Bolstler

Rick was born in Edmonton, Alberta, Canada in 1944. He graduated from the University of Alberta with a degree in Mathematics and began his career with IBM Canada in Ottawa in 1966. In 1978 he left IBM and Ottawa, moving to Vancouver. He met his wife Heather, married in 1979 and had 2 children, Michael and Jennifer. In 1983 Rick and his family emigrated to Australia, choosing Sydney as their new home. Soon the family became Australian citizens. Rick and Heather started a computer training company which they ran together until 2003, when they sold it to a competitor. In 2008 Rick and Heather retired, moving from Sydney to Mitchells Island where they built a home and continue to reside.

rbolstler@gmail.com

Desley Polmear

Desley Polmear lives in Wauchope NSW. Her passions are writing, singing, the arts, live concerts, plays and travelling. '*Shattered*' is her fourth novel following her best-selling murder mystery trilogy. *"Unlocked Secrets," "Just before Midnight"* and *"Payback."*

Desley sings with Sing Australia on Thursdays and often attends nursing homes to sing to the elderly folk.

Desley writes over 500 words a day when she is not travelling around the globe. When she gets the time she loves painting in watercolours. She runs workshops helping others to begin their passion of writing a novel or perhaps their memoir.

www.desleypolmearcreative.com

Barbara Edmunds

It is a love of words which drew me to Scribblers. I wanted to know the myriad ways they could rub against each other and still retain meaning. Unlike many of the members who make up the whole of the group, I was unpublished and deeply inexperienced. I had done a creative writing course, which gave me invaluable insights into the many theories as to how others write creatively, but little practice in using these theories to create my own imaginings.

Thanks to Scribblers I have now had a one thousand word story included in Volume 4 of the Seniors Stories. It pales in comparison to the achievements of others within the group, but for me it represents the end of a lifetime of dreaming. I am now an out there and proud published author!

Robin Sheppard

Robin considers herself an artist more than a writer, but enjoys reading all types of written work. Around 2015, she and her daughter Jenny Trotter, who has an interest in writing stories, attended their first Scribblers meeting and although being a bit at sea, continued to attend meetings after that. Robin decided to educate herself further in the art of writing by learning editing and proof reading and digital illustration. With the knowledge gained from that, Scribblers workshops and writing prompt word stories, she and Jen worked together on a children's book and it was first published in 2019.

Michael Davies

Michael was an avid reader from the age of five and spent a significant part of his life in libraries. Challenged to write a novel at the age of 43, he wrote a murder mystery of 100,000 words, but it was dreadful. After four more such works, *"Dreamkill,"* a psychological thriller was published in the USA. All his subsequent works have been self-published. Of his 28 books, 16 have been written as collaborative projects with schoolchildren, mostly in the 8-13 age group. The adult books are in the sci-fi, political thriller and murder mystery genres. One of these, *"The Janus Conspiracy"* a political thriller is under review by a Hollywood producer for a possible movie. Michael has also been an active publisher for other writers, with more than 85 books published. He has travelled a great deal, having lived and worked in the UK, Canada, Australia, the USA and South-East Asia.

Heather Bolstler

I haven't always been writing but I've always been a writer. I fashioned poetry, short stories and spellbinding novels as a teenager, graduating to essays at university and stage plays while teaching high school drama. As a full-time mum my medium was letter writing. While running a corporate training company based in Sydney and Melbourne, I evolved into writing and editing copy, world-class proposal responses, and course manuals. Finally, in retirement I began to satisfy a long-suppressed craving for short story writing.

Amidst all this, there was book, Shedders, written to tell the unusual tale of how I and my five housemates came to set up a communal household in the heart of the Manning Valley. This memoir sits on Amazon Books, patiently selling a copy now and then despite no marketing whatever.

My writing, and that of others, has given my life a perfect self-expression.

https://shedders.wordpress.com/

Maureen Larter

Maureen was born in England in the late 1940's and came over to Australia when still a toddler. She is a teacher of piano and violin, and lives on the lower Mid North Coast of New South Wales, Australia. She lives on a small-holding of 12 acres, and does her best to live self-sufficiently, while taking care of the soil and the environment. In the past, she has taught English, Social Studies, Music and Mathematics in High Schools within Australia, as well as living in China for a short time, teaching English. She has also taught in Cambodia. On wet days, when she can't be out in her garden, and there are no students commandeering her time, she loves to sit and write. She writes children's stories and short stories, as well as occasional articles for magazines.

She has recently (under the pen-name Marguerite Wellbourne) branched out into adult drama.

A children's chapter book about elves:
http://amzn.com/B00BLVP0KM
My fan page on
Facebook: www.facebook.com/eBooksByMaureenLarter
My author page on
Amazon: http://www.amazon.com/-/e/B00ISCNZ4U

Avril Brown

In my youth I was a regular writer and have always enjoyed putting pen to paper. A love of the written word led me to study languages and I spent many months in France acquiring a thorough knowledge of French and also travelled to India and attended conferences to learn Sanskrit and some classical Latin.

I have always found it a great help to collaborate with others and belonged to a writing group in 1983 as a young mum. Gradually, career commitments and child-rearing took over my daily schedule, leaving little or no time for writing.

Running my own Sydney-based business in the intervening 20 years provided ample opportunity for writing business documents, reports and correspondence, yet I missed the pleasures of creative writing.

Moving from Sydney to the Mid North Coast in 2011 provided a slowdown in the pace of life, and I joined Taree Scribblers early in 2019 after a long hiatus.

From this association with other writers, I look forward to returning to a pastime which has always provided great pleasure in my life.

Eve Grzybowski

Eve Grzybowski has been teaching for 30-plus years, practising yoga continuously since 1971, and training yoga teachers since the mid-nineties. Besides yoga, writing is a passion. She has written two published books, many yoga-related articles, and her pet– "*Yoga Suits Her*" – a weekly blog. Her memoir is a work in progress. Eve has written a no-nonsense, jargon-free book on yoga for novices and those with experience, too. There are chapters on motivation, breathing techniques, getting started, and how to cope with stress in your daily life.

Rae-Lee Diamond

Rae-lee moved to the Manning Valley with her daughter in 2012 from the Central Coast. It took some courage plucking for this poet to join Taree Scribblers seven years later, hoping to gain some confidence and encouragement in her poetry writing, to expand into short stories and essays as well as get moving with a book floating around in her head. Rae-lee entered her first poetry competition *"The Manning in Rhyme"* in 2016 and received the Hans Ruiner Encouragement Award for her poem *"In Country Wingham"*. Rae-lee thoroughly enjoys interacting with the other Scribblers and especially loves the workshops each month.

Melissa Haigh

Connecting ideas and surfacing recurrent themes holds an eternal fascination for Mim Haigh. She writes professionally, personally and creatively.

Jacqueline Winn

Jacqueline lives on a farm at Possum Brush on the Mid-North Coast of NSW. She writes short stories, novels, poetry and scripts and has won awards for short story and poetry in Australia, New Zealand and UK. A number of her stories have been published in anthologies and literary magazines in Australia, UK and Ireland. She has two collections of short stories *"Once More With Feeling"* and *"Salt & Pepper,"* published by Ginninderra Press. More about Jacqui and her writing at www.jacquelinewinn.com

Bob Winston

Although I remember enjoying writing stories from an early age my breakthrough did not happen until I was sixteen. Two prizes of five pounds each were announced for best submissions to the Nowra school magazine *"Shoalhaven"*. A poem and a short story were required. I decided to win both.

I did but only one 'literature' prize was awarded. That was the beginning of the deception. Instead of a five pound note I was given one five pound gift voucher to be redeemed at the local bookshop.

At the bookshop I was invited to select books to the value of the prize. They would be sent to the headmaster for his approval before being endorsed by him then presented at Speech Day.

Steinbeck was very fashionable at the time. I chose *"East of Eden."* Kylie Tennant was also the talk of the era. I chose *"The Joyful Condemned"*. My third choice was *"Coonadoo"* by Katharine Susannah Pritchard because I was interested in aboriginal issues.

Headmaster was outraged. He refused to put the school's name to leftist views of Steinbeck or Tennant. Little did he know Katharine Susannah Pritchard was a raving Communist or he would have banned *"Coonardoo"* also. Mum bought the banned books for me and I skipped Speech Night in silent protest. It would be another sixteen years before I picked up my pen again.

Nyngan had a struggling little writers group which I joined after winning The Gold Pen Award at Nyngan Agricultural Show in 1970 something. It was a gold plated biro that I was very proud of.

I was secretary of Nyngan Branch of The United Farmers and Wool Growers Association. I kept the minutes with my gold plated pen until one night I passed around the attendance sheet with it. The attendance sheet returned with a plastic pen but I did not notice that until the next day. I was seriously pissed off but never recovered my gold pen. I hope someone gets guilty, sleepless nights over that theft.

We retired to Taree district in 2002. I busied myself with all things agricultural but that ancient need to write had not gone away. I looked about for a writers club but there was none. The upshot was 'SCRIBBLERS'.

Kerry MacAulay

A passion for words, an enduring love of reading and a fancy for writing poetry and short stories are some of the reasons why Kerry MacAulay is a member of Taree Scribblers. She has completed a couple of academic theses but otherwise has yet to be published.

Joan Stanfield

Some years of study and scholarship passed before I once again took up the challenge to write. This time I picked up the gauntlet, with a contract as a radio news reporter for ABC Newcastle. At this time I had an enthusiastic editor who gave me encouragement.

With the beginning of Channel 3 Television in the beginning of the 1960s, my husband a keen photographer upgraded his movie camera and became the North Coast Stringer Cameraman. This became more than 20 years of filming for Ch 3 and shortly afterwards, ABC news Sydney. Thus began a family commitment. I worked on shot-listing, and the scripting of stories sourced by us.

During my 23 years of teaching, at secondary level, many hours of writing, specifically for Art History, demanded research, time and rewrites at a period well before computer support.

After the beginning of video and electronic transmission in the 1980s, we took on other challenges, after many years of teaching we retrained and took on the challenge of our travel business, offering divergence of writing for itineraries to fulfil clients' dreams.

My continued genealogical research progressed to compiling stories. I was recommended to contain them into book form, but it wasn't until the freedom of retirement, allowed me to get down to serious writing. Now with four books published, to date, I need to keep writing.

It is my current challenge and therapy. My publisher nominated me for the Non-Fiction section of the Walkleys 2015. The nomination was accepted and last week I was invited to the Long List/Short List finals in Sydney Oct 22.

My eldest daughter. a designer, represented me. I was chuffed to be in august company but didn't get into the Final 10, from which the winner will be announced in Melbourne in beginning of Dec.

The book, my third, *"Border Pioneers...the Pastoralists,"* described the lives of men who braved the unknown from 1840s, exploring the great river systems of the Clarence and Richmond, Logan and Condamine, developing land leased and purchased as registered working land owners. They left their mark on Australian history.

First book: *"A Patchwork Quilt,"* a Pioneering Saga. From the First Fleet onwards, the early pioneers, convict and free settlers bonded by mate-ship and inter-marriage stitched together the fabric of nationhood.

Book 2: *"Jennings Quest..the Riddle of the Notebook,"* follows the discovery of a 100 year old hand written book about an unsigned Will which was contested as the longest Court Case in British legal history, known as the Great Jennings Case.

Book 4: *"ABIGAIL..a Chance Encounter"* is a mid-life romance, threatening her trust as she was exposed to ingenuous and gratuitous advice, over, the erosion of her investments.

Les Eastaway

Les is a third generation Australian, his great grandfather coming from Ireland.

Taree is his home-town and following an almost lifetime of employment in Sydney he returned to live out his years in the Manning.

Numerous sports were a focal point growing up with his love of cricket a clear favourite choice. The written word was also an attraction with contributions to two country newspapers filing stories and results for cricket associations. A short stint behind the microphone on a radio sports show held fond memories.

He wrote newsletters for various cricket clubs and a dedicated few years leading into retirement resulted in penning a comprehensive book. "Cricket in the Manning" showcased a one hundred and twenty year history of sport in the region. Copies of the book have reached readers in all states of Australia along with New Zealand and Hong Kong. Still connected to the sport, he is Treasurer of the MRD Cricket Association. The art of Bonsai is also an interesting and diverse hobby. Movies and live theatre round out his interests with grandchildren a daily reminder of *"ain't life grand"*.

www.ingramcontent.com/pod-product-compliance
Lightning Source LLC
Chambersburg PA
CBHW070419120726
47909CB00005B/1713